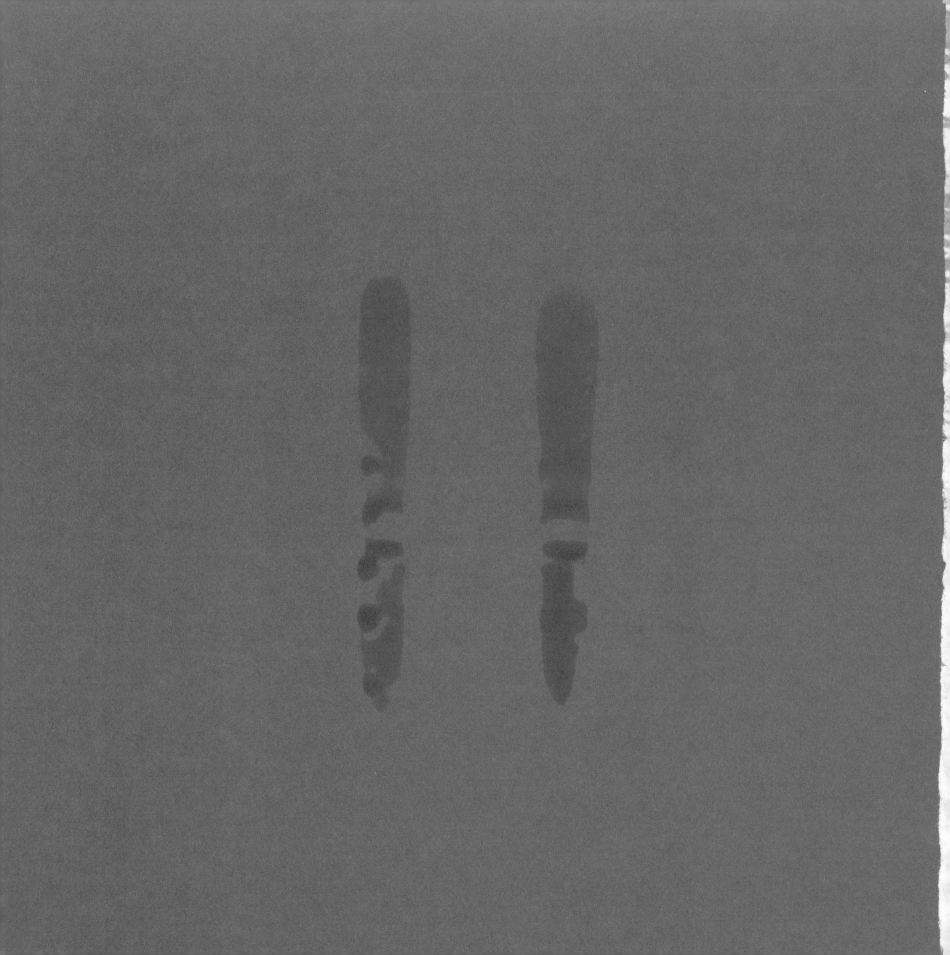

GLORIA RAND

Baby in a Basket

Illustrated by TED RAND

COBBLEHILL BOOKS / Dutton · New York

Dedicated to Ann Jeffries and Betty Peth,
the real baby Ann and her big sister, Betty

Text copyright © 1997 by Gloria Rand
Illustrations copyright © 1997 by Ted Rand

Library of Congress Cataloging-in-Publication Data
Rand, Gloria.
Baby in a basket / Gloria Rand;
illustrated by Ted Rand.   p.   cm.
Summary: In 1917, Marie and her children Betty
and baby Ann are leaving Alaska for the winter by
sleigh, when disaster strikes during a snowstorm.
ISBN 0-525-65233-7
[1. Alaska—Fiction.   2. Accidents—Fiction.
3. Babies—Fiction.]   I. Rand, Ted, ill.   II. Title.
PZ7.R1553Bab 1997 [Fic]—dc20 96-33805 CIP AC

Published in the United States by Cobblehill Books,
an affiliate of Dutton Children's Books,
a division of Penguin USA, Inc.
375 Hudson Street, New York, New York 10014
Designed by Kathleen Westray
Printed in Hong Kong
First Edition   10 9 8 7 6 5 4 3 2 1

AUTHOR'S NOTE

In mid-January, 1917, Marie Boyer, Fairbanks, Alaska's first kindergarten teacher, left central Alaska to stay with relatives in Seattle, Washington, until spring. With her were her daughters, three-year-old Betty and four-month-old baby Ann.

They were embarking on a journey that meant traveling for ten days in an open sleigh, then proceeding on south for five days aboard a steamship.

Edward Howard Boyer, husband and father, remained at his job as the postmaster of Fairbanks.

Tragedy struck early in the trip when the sleigh carrying Marie and her children crashed into the Delta River near Donnelly's roadhouse.

This story is based on their adventure.

"THERE YA GO, little traveler." Mr. McNutt lifted a small basket up onto the back seat of his sleigh. In the basket, all cuddly and warm under soft furs, was baby Ann.

"Now, Missie, it's your turn." The sleigh driver smiled as he lifted Ann's big sister, Betty, up onto the same back seat and put her down next to her mother.

"I want you girls to ride close to your Ma," he explained, as he tucked all three into a nest of woolly blankets and fur throws. "It's going to be a mighty cold trip, maybe a little bumpy too. Best you stay snuggled together."

Ann, Betty, and their mother, Marie, were leaving Alaska, leaving the bitter cold and the dark days of winter in the far north. In spring, when the weather turned warmer and the days lighter, they would return.

Ann's father looked concerned, "Take care. Have a safe journey." He kissed each of them good-bye.

Then, as six huge horses pulled the sleigh out of town, sleigh bells ringing and the horses' hooves making loud crunchy sounds in the snow, he swung a lighted lantern in farewell.

Marie had prepared carefully for this journey. She had lined

a basket with heavy canvas to make a protected cradle for
baby Ann. She had knit each girl red wool leggings with
mittens to match, and mended their hand-me-down tiny fur
coats and hats. She borrowed extra blankets to have in the
sleigh. She washed out a big thermos bottle to carry heated
milk in, for them to drink along the way.

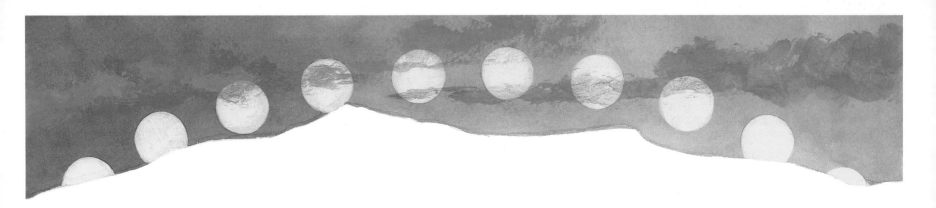

The three travelers, along with two other passengers, rode from early morning until late at night, up into high mountains, then down across stretches of land that was low. They rode mostly in the dark, as there was little daylight that far north in the winter. They rode sometimes under clear starry skies, more often through fog, sleet, and falling snow.

When she wasn't napping Ann chewed on her mittens and played with her baby rattle.

Betty kept busy singing songs to her teddy bear, and often asked where they were going, and how long it would be before they got there.

As they sped along the lonely wilderness trail, Mr. McNutt often called back to his little passengers, even though he knew baby Ann was too young to understand, "Lookee, lookee over there, girls. See Mr. Fox, that's him, by golly. See his fluffy tail?"

When a snowy owl swooped near the sleigh, or a snowshoe rabbit came their way, Mr. McNutt spotted them too. He had very sharp eyes.

At the end of every day Mr. McNutt stopped the sleigh at a roadhouse, one of many small lodges along the trail, each placed one day's travel from the next. In these roadhouses everyone ate a hot dinner and bedded down for a good night's sleep. Ann always had warm milk and cereal. Everyone else

had bacon and bean soup or wild game stew. There was
cake for dessert and often dried fruit pie, too. After they had
traveled for several days the weather became dark and stormy.
The wind howled and the snow now blew in blinding swirls.
It was very cold.

Nearing the Delta River, at the end of a long day, the wind began to blow even harder, rocking the sleigh from side to side. Marie held tightly onto the basket Ann was in, and just as tightly onto Betty.

As the sleigh neared a narrow log bridge, close to the roadhouse where they were to stop for the night, the horses bolted. In a panic the lead horse raced off the bridge and plunged through the ice that covered the river. The other horses and the sleigh followed in a terrible crash that scattered passengers, luggage, blankets, and fur throws in every direction.

"Where are they? Where are my babies?" Marie cried out as she tried to stand. "Help me! Somebody help me find my children!"

It was nearly impossible to see through the swirling snow, and the wind was blowing so hard no one, not even Mr. McNutt, could stay standing. Frantically everyone crawled across the ice looking for Betty and Ann. "Over there! Over there!" sharp-eyed Mr. McNutt shouted above the screeching wind. "There's something red over there!"

It was Betty's legging caught on the edge of the ice that covered the river. Betty was trapped under the ice, only her legging was keeping her from being swept on downstream.

She was blue with cold and choking when Mr. McNutt pulled her from the icy water and quickly wrapped her in a blanket.

The desperate search for Ann continued. Where was she?

The searchers quickly became exhausted and chilled to the bone, their damp clothing frozen stiff as planks.

"We have to get to the roadhouse right now!" Mr. McNutt shouted. "If we don't get into a shelter soon, we're all going to freeze to death. We're all going to die!"

"But my baby, my baby," Marie pleaded. "I have to find my baby!"

The idea of leaving Ann out in the storm was too horrible to even imagine. Marie collapsed.

Unable to stand in the strong wind, the two passengers made their way to the roadhouse on their hands and knees, dragging Marie with them. Mr. McNutt followed, dragging Betty.

Once inside Marie clung to Betty and wept, too stunned
by the loss of baby Ann to speak.

The roadhouse owner quickly put on his warmest clothing
and headed out by himself to look for Ann. No one else, not
even Mr. McNutt, had enough strength left to go back out
with him.

Huddled around the fireplace, the travelers waited and
silently worried. Where was the owner? Why hadn't he come
back yet? Was he lost too? What about Ann?

When the roadhouse owner returned, he returned alone.

"Please, can't you go back out with me? I'm stronger now
and I have to find my baby," Marie sobbed. "I have to find her."

At that moment the front door burst open. Following a blast of cold air, in staggered two snow-covered men carrying a snow-covered basket.

At the sight of the basket Marie gasped and nearly collapsed again.

"That's my baby's basket. Is she in there?"

"This here your little baby, Ma'am?" one of the men proudly asked as he brushed snow off the covering of fur that had been protecting Ann from the cold. "We was crossin' the river on downstream aways, when we saw this little ol' basket sailin' along on top of the ice."

Marie reached for the basket, weeping tears of joy at the sight of baby Ann, dry, warm, and unhurt.

"Didn't know there was a baby missing," the other man explained. "Thought this here was just a basket with furs. Two old trappers like us couldn't let a basket of furs go by, now could we? Grabbed hold, and durn it all if a little red mitten didn't wave out at us."

The roadhouse filled with hoots and hollers of happiness.

Ann was passed from person to person. Everyone wanted to hold the baby, everyone except Betty, who was busy racing around in crazy excited circles.

That evening, in celebration, the roadhouse owner played the fiddle, his wife and Mr. McNutt sang, and the passengers

danced an Irish jig, while the two old trappers kept a watchful eye on Ann, who was sleeping peacefully by the fire.

"There she was, ridin' on downriver," they kept repeating in wonder. "Hard to believe, but there she was, a beautiful baby in that there basket."

The next day, after the six huge horses had been rounded up, the travelers were once again on their way, riding in a sledge that had been found to replace the wrecked sleigh.